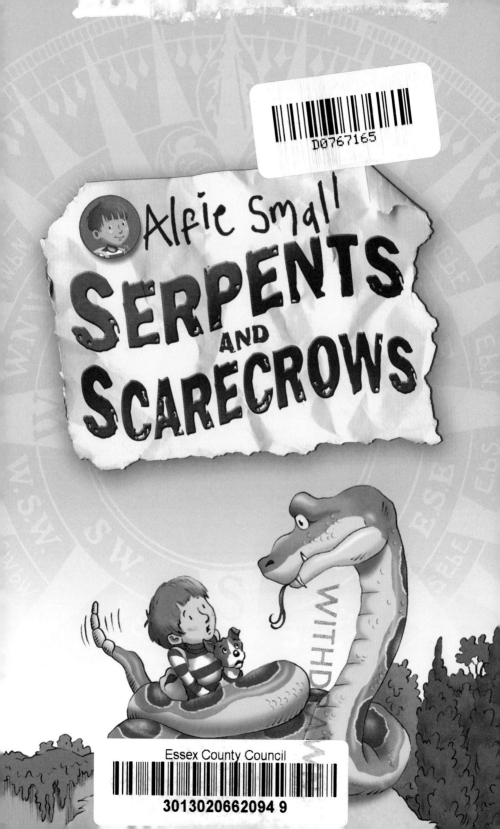

Alfie Small
SERPENTS AND SCARECROWS

Mum,
I have gone exploring.
Got my rucksack. Don't
worry, I'll be home in
time for tea. Love,
Alfie X

Here's the note I always
leave for Mum before I go
on another adventure

ADVENTURE
HOME
Alfie Small

ALFIE SMALL JOURNAL 3: Serpents And Scarecrows
A DAVID FICKLING BOOK 978 1 849 92121 3

Published in Great Britain by David Fickling Books,
a division of Random House Children's Publishers UK
A Random House Group Company

This edition published 2013

1 3 5 7 9 10 8 6 4 2

Copyright © Alfie Small, 2013

DAVID FICKLING BOOKS
31 Beaumont Street, Oxford, OX1 2NP

www.randomhousechildrens.co.uk
www.totallyrandombooks.co.uk
www.randomhouse.co.uk

Addresses for companies within The Random House Group Limited can be found at:
www.randomhouse.co.uk/offices.htm

THE RANDOM HOUSE GROUP Limited Reg. No. 954009

A CIP catalogue record for this book is available from the British Library.

Printed in China

Photographs of Alfie's finds by Ian Rycroft. www.ianrycroft.co.uk

This is the Adventure Journal of

Alfie Small

Hobbies: Exploring and having adventures!

My best friend: Jed

Things I Like: Slithering snakes and
fat, furry voles

Things I Hate: Scary scarecrows and
man-eating plants

1. Down We Go!

This is me

Jed →

This is my explorer's kit

My name is Alfie Small, and this is my brave dog, Jed. I'm a famous explorer and have lots of dangerous adventures. I always take my rucksack with me, just in case!

At the bottom of my garden, behind the rickety shed, is the special place I go exploring. The grass is long and the weeds grow thick and I never know what I might find.

Corkscrew
nose cone

Caterpillar
tracks

Today, I pushed through the weeds
. . . and found a very strange machine
indeed. It had caterpillar tracks and a
corkscrew nose.

"Come on, Jed," I cried, opening the
door and climbing inside. Jed leaped
in beside me. I pressed a button, the
engines roared into life and the strange
machine lurched forward.

The corkscrew nose started to turn, and before I knew what was happening, the machine began tunnelling into the earth.

"Yippee! Here we go, Jed," I cheered, but Jed looked rather nervous as we disappeared below the ground.

"Wooaah!" he whined.

We burrowed deeper and deeper, turning this way and that. Soon, all I could see was the tip of the corkscrew nose, glowing red in the dark as it sliced through the rocky earth.

"Oh no!" I cried. "It's starting to overheat." Then, as the digger began to climb, its engines clattered and groaned. *Clang, Whirr!*

"Don't stop now," I begged.

I turned the throttle, the screw span even faster and we burst out of the ground into the dazzling sunshine of a wild, unkempt garden.

"Phew, made it," I sighed, as the digger came to a halt in a cloud of steam. It started to judder and shake.

"Let's get out of here," I yelled. "It's going to blow!" Grabbing Jed in my arms, I dived from the digger.

BOOM! The machine exploded and we were sent flying through the air.

"Help!" I cried.

"Wooaah!" howled Jed. We landed
with a thump on something soft.

"Phew! That was lucky," I said. But
I had spoken too soon, because we'd
dropped straight into the twisting coils
of a gigantic snake.

Yikes!

2. Snakes Alive!

"SSSSS!" hissed the fork-tongued serpent. "I'll ssqueeze you until you ssqueak, you insssufferable ssquirts!"

"Let go," I gasped, feeling his thick, scaly body tighten around me. "I'm not a tube of toothpaste."

"Won't!" snapped the bad-tempered snake, tightening his grip even more.

"Agh!" I gasped, and pulling one hand free, I reached into my rucksack. I took out a packet of itching powder, tore off the corner and sprinkled it over the serpent's scaly back.

"Sss-sss-sss-sssstop," hissed the snake as he burst into uncontrollable giggles, and began to wriggle and squirm like a worm on a hook. Jed and I jumped from his writhing coils and ran behind a rock for cover.

My cousin Charlie gave me this bag of itching powder. It's really itchy!

"Ooh, ah, ooh!" cried the serpent, twitching and wiggling. Then, as we watched, a most curious thing happened. His old skin started to come off like a dirty sock.

Underneath he was as bright as fresh paint. "Ahhhhh!" sighed the snake as his frantic wriggling stopped. "Oh, bliss! What was that marvellous medicine?" he asked. "I've been trying to shed my sssskin for ages. Thank you."

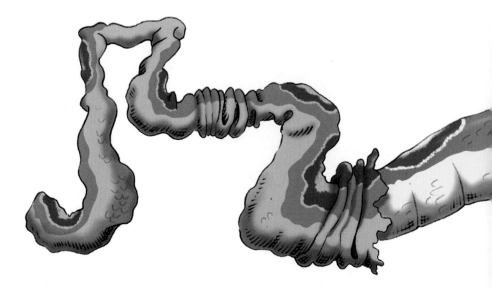

"That's OK," I said, stepping out
warily from behind the rock.

"Don't be sscared," hissed the snake.
"I don't bite. I was just in a bit of a mood.
It gets sso uncomfortable when your
sskin's too tight!" He slid up beside me.
"My name's Sssamson. Who are you?"

"I'm Alfie Small, the famous explorer,"
I said.

"Well, if you're ever in trouble, Alfie, just
shout and I'll come a-sssslithering. OK?"

"Thanks, Samson," I said, patting his nose. "Cheerio. We've got to get going."

"Bye Alfie, and watch out for the Ssscarecrow," hissed Samson.

"What scarecrow?" I asked, but the snake had already slinked off into the undergrowth.

What a strange thing to say, I thought. I mean, how scary can a scarecrow be?

3. Snared

"Come on, Jed. Let's go," I called, but when I looked around, he wasn't there. He had skedaddled!

"Oh no, he's up to his old tricks again," I sighed. "Jed, where are you? Come here," I yelled, following a grassy track deeper into the overgrown garden.

I hadn't gone far when I saw clusters of fat blackberries hanging from a branch above me. My tummy rumbled with hunger. I picked a handful and stuffed them into my mouth.

Mmm, they were delicious. But as I reached out to pick some more, I felt something grip my ankle. I looked down and saw a thick plant stem wrapping itself around my leg.

Oops, I got some berry juice on ← my book

"Hey, what's going on?" I cried in alarm and kicked out. Then another tendril wriggled through the air, curling around my wrist and holding me tight. Oh, yikes! I tugged with all my might, but it was no good. I was trapped!

In a panic, I grabbed the dinosaur's tooth out of my rucksack. I'd collected it on my last adventure, and it was as sharp as an axe. I chopped at the sinewy stalks around my tethered wrist, slicing them in two. I did the same to the twitching tendrils binding my ankles. With a snap they parted, and I jumped free.

"Phew! That was close!" I cried, my heart pounding.

As I hurried away, an angry bark sounded in the distance. It was Jed. Something had happened to him.

"Where are you, boy?" I called, trying to pinpoint the sound. It seemed to be coming from a nearby wood. "Coming, Jed."

4. Wilfred's Tale

I followed a track into the spooky wood. It led me on a winding course between twisted trunks. I began to hear noises in the undergrowth and shuddered, imagining horrific beasts hiding behind every tree.

"Wooah!" Jed howled, very close by.

Maybe a marauding monster has got him, I thought, and started to run. I came to a clearing in the trees. The ground was covered with a thick carpet of bindweed.

Has a marauding monster got Jed?

I was trapped!

"Where are you, Jed?" I shouted.
He had to be here somewhere, but I
couldn't see him.

"JED! – Arrrgh!" I cried, as the
bindweed gave way and I dropped into
a pit in the ground. With a rustling
noise, the stringy weed started to grow
back, weaving itself into a strong mesh
and trapping me in the hole.

"What is it with the plants in this
place?" I groaned.

"Woof!" yapped Jed, leaping into my lap and licking my face.

"So there you are, boy," I said, rubbing his grubby coat. "That'll teach you to run off. Now, let's get out of here."

"Eek! No ch-ch-chance of that," said a piping, tremulous voice. "We're all d-d-doomed!"

I glanced up and saw a fat, furry rodent, crouching in the shadows.

"Who are you?" I asked, in surprise.

"W-W-Wilfred the water vole," he squealed, twitching his whiskers and shaking like a furry jelly.

W-W-Wilfred

"Don't worry, Wilfred. I'm Alfie Small, the famous explorer," I said. "I'll soon get us out of here." I took the scissors from my rucksack and tried to snip through the bindweed. It was no good – it was as tough as wire. "Darn it!"

"T-t-told you," stammered Wilfred, wringing his paws. "The creepy Scarecrow's got us, and we're all d-d-doomed."

"You mean we're prisoners of the Scarecrow?" I gasped, my blood running cold.

Wilfred nodded, his little black eyes shining with fear. I felt so stupid. Samson had warned me about the Scarecrow, and now I was caught in one of his traps!

I warned you!

"He's the t-t-terrible tyrant that rules the whole g-g-garden," continued the vole. "He's f-f-frightened all the birds away, and feeds morsels like us to his gi-g-g-gantic prize bloom."

"Whoa, hold on a bit," I said. "A plant can't eat us!"

"This one can," sobbed the vole.

Poor Uncle Roderick, eaten by a plant!

"It's already eaten my Uncle Roderick."

"Crikey! We've got to get out of here," I gulped, reaching up and tugging desperately at the bindweed.

"T-t-too late!" squealed Wilfred, for now we could hear the sound of tiny marching feet and the shuffling of much larger footsteps. "We're all d-d-doooomed!"

Suddenly, the marching stopped. A shadow fell across us, and a horrible face peered through the mesh.

"Well, well," said the Scarecrow in a rasping whisper. "Look what's fallen into my trap. Good thing my Precious is so hungry. Hee-hee-hee."

Uh-oh!

5. The Scarecrow

The Scarecrow's head was a worm-eaten sack stuffed with straw. He had a large felt nose, piercing painted eyes and a jagged tear for a mouth.

"Clear off," I demanded. "No one is using me for plant food!"

"Quiet, human!" croaked the Scarecrow with a sneer. "You're trespassing in my garden, and must pay the ultimate price."

With a clap of his straw hands, the bindweed unravelled. A row of flowers, walking on their muddy roots, clustered around the edge of the hole. Their petals were shaped like beaks and edged with jagged teeth.

"S-s-snapdragons," sobbed Wilfred, as the flowers leaped down beside us, snapping like wild things. Jed growled menacingly, but he was outnumbered, and was forced to scramble up the sloping side of the crater with the quivering vole.

The Scarecrow reached down, grabbed me by my collar and hauled me out. I tried to break free, but even though he was made of straw, he was immensely strong. He pinched my cheek with his scratchy fingers. "Yes, my Precious is going to enjoy eating you. Hee-hee-hee," he giggled.

"Let me go, you overgrown muppet," I hollered, but the Scarecrow ignored me.

"Take them to the arena," he ordered gruffly. Surrounded by the snapping flowers, Jed and Wilfred were herded out of the clearing and down a narrow path. The Scarecrow dragged me along behind them.

Oh yikes!

6. Man-eater!

The path led us into a musty, dripping gorge. Poison ivy clung to the tall rocky sides, and nearly covered the mouth of a large cave at the bottom. In front of the cave stood two wooden posts with ropes hanging from them. Bleached bones were scattered across the ground.

The musty gorge

As the flowers formed a guard around us, the Scarecrow tied me to one post, and Jed and Wilfred to the other.

"I'll get you for this, sawdust brain," I said, struggling against my bonds, but the straw man just laughed.

"Dinner is served, my Precious," he cried. "Come and get it!"

Everything went creepily quiet. Then a slow, shuffling noise sounded inside the cave and a rotten stench filled the air. The poison ivy parted as the most enormous plant I've ever seen crawled out into the open, like a revolting giant slug.

"Yikes!" I cried, desperately trying to undo the knots around my wrists. If only I could reach my dinosaur tooth.

Jed growled and Wilfred whined.

Then, as the fetid plant crawled closer, we froze in terror. Its large, fleshy jowls rippled as it opened an enormous crimson mouth. It bent down and sniffed each one of us in turn.

We needed help, fast!

"SAMSON!" I shouted at the top of my voice.

"No one can help you now, you snivelling weevil," cackled the Scarecrow. "Come on, Precious, tuck in!"

The plant struck, snapping the post that held Jed and Wilfred. It lifted them into the air, dangling on the ends of their ropes. Then, with a slurping noise, the plant sucked the ropes up like strings of spaghetti.

Slurp!

Jed's rope broke and he fell to the
ground, but the poor vole disappeared
into the plant's drooling jaws.

Snarling with fury, Jed attacked,
sinking his teeth into the monster's thick
stem. With a horrible gurgle, the plant
spat Wilfred out. It made a grab for Jed,
but my brave dog darted out of reach.

"Don't let them escape!" roared the Scarecrow as a dazed Wilfred landed with a bump, and the circle of Snapdragons darted about trying to round up my two friends.

Now, the giant plant loomed over me. It shook its leaves in frustration and opened its dribbling mouth as wide as a whale's. I closed my eyes in terror!

"Finish him off, Precious!" cackled the Scarecrow.

7. A Mighty Battle

I heard a familiar hiss and the rustle of leaves, and opened my eyes to see Samson slithering out of the bushes towards us. The Snapdragons took one look and fled, shedding their petals in fear. But the giant plant turned to face the hissing serpent.

"I'll crush the sssap out of you, you overgrown weed," said Samson, and the two enemies set upon each other, wrapping themselves into a writhing tangle of coils and roots. They wrestled and squeezed and snapped and hissed.

"Go, Samson, go!" I cheered as my fingers finally prised open the knots and my bonds slipped to the ground.

"Leave my Precious alone!" cried the Scarecrow, pulling a colossal thorn from his pocket and rushing to attack the slippery snake. I dived through the air and knocked him to the ground, sending his weapon spinning out of reach.

I grappled with the furious Scarecrow but he was too strong and he bent my arms back and pinned me to the ground.

The thorn

"Got you!" he growled. "I'll turn you
into compost, you grovelling grub!"

"Grrrr!" Jed dived at the Scarecrow,
clamping his teeth around his bulbous
nose, and tugging for all he was worth.

"B-b-bash him, Jed," squealed Wilfred,
hiding halfway up a nearby tree.

"Ged off by dose!" growled the
struggling Scarecrow, but Jed pulled
even harder and the nose started to
stretch. "I said, ged off by ..." But
then, with a loud *RIP!* the Scarecrow's

head came right off, and the stuffing inside was scattered to the wind. The Scarecrow went as limp as a rag doll.

"Phew! Thanks, Jed," I gasped, as a flock of birds appeared, twittering and chirruping in delight. They gathered beakfuls of the Scarecrow's straw and darted off to build their nests.

All of a sudden, *Crunch!* A terrific noise split the air as Samson gave his opponent an almighty squeeze. The giant plant's stem snapped in two and it collapsed to the ground.

"Yessssss!" hissed the serpent in triumph.
"Yeehah! Well done, Samson!" I crowed.
"W-w-well done, all of you," cried Wilfred, stammering with excitement as he scampered across to join us. "Now we

can all live safely in the garden."

Just then, a delicious smell, from far, far away, drifted through the air. I lifted my nose and sniffed. "Mmm, my tea's ready," I said. "I need to get home, but my digger is kaput!"

"Don't concern yoursssself, Alfie. I have a plan!" hissed Samson.

I kept some actual straw from the scarecrow!

8. Crazy Catapults!

The snake wrapped his tail around a tree trunk, then reached out and grabbed another tree in his mouth.

"Now ssstretch my tummy back as far as it will go," mumbled Samson.

Wilfred · Jed and me · Tree stump · String · Samson!

Wilfred, Jed and I pulled, and pulled, and pulled the middle of his body until it would stretch no more. Then we tied it to a tree stump with some string from my rucksack.

Jed and I sat on the serpent's quivering middle and held on tight.

"Bye Wilfred. Bye Samson," I said.

"So long, Alfie," hissed Samson. "NOW!" he yelled and Wilfred snipped through the string with his teeth. *Twang!* Samson's body shot forwards like elastic, and Jed and I were catapulted up over the treetops.

"Thank you, Alfie. Thank you, Jed," called Wilfred, and then we were lost from sight.

Whoosh! We fell from the sky and landed in a patch of thick, springy grass. Scrambling to my feet, I pushed through the tall and tangled weeds and came out from behind the shed at the bottom of my garden.

"Alfie, your tea is ready," I heard Mum call. "It's fish and chips."

Mmmm, that's my favourite – but I hope we don't have blackberry pie for afters!

"C'mon, Jed," I cried and we raced up the garden path.

I am Alfie Small, the famous explorer, and I can't wait for my next adventure to begin.